Disney PRINCESS

Sleeping Beauty

Read-and-Sing

DiSNEP PRESS

New York • Los Angeles

For information address Disney Press, 1101 Flower Street, Glendale, California 91201.

ISBN 978-1-4847-0431-8
F383-2370-2-14122
Printed in China
First Edition
1 3 5 7 9 10 8 6 4 2

For more Disney Press fun visit www.disneybooks.com

Contents

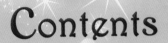

Sleeping Beauty

Long ago, in a faraway land, King Stefan and his fair queen wished for a child. Finally, their wish was granted and a daughter was born. They named her Aurora.

To honor the baby princess, the king held a great feast. Nobles, peasants, knights, and ladies all joyfully flocked to the castle.

King Stefan welcomed his good friend King Hubert to the feast. King Hubert brought his young son, Phillip, with him. The two kings, who wished to unite their kingdoms, agreed that someday Phillip and Aurora would be married.

Among the guests were three good fairies: Flora, Fauna, and Merryweather. Each of them wished to bless the infant with a gift.

Waving her wand, Flora chanted, "My gift shall be the gift of Beauty."

"And mine," said Fauna, "shall be the gift of Song."

Merryweather's turn was next. But before she could
speak, the castle doors flew open. A tiny flame appeared and
grew into the form of the evil fairy Maleficent. Maleficent
was angry that she hadn't been invited to the feast.

"I, too, have a gift for the newborn babe," she said with a
sneer. "She shall indeed grow in grace and beauty. But before
the sun sets on her sixteenth birthday, she shall prick her
finger on the spindle of a spinning wheel . . . and die!"

Then, with a cruel laugh, the evil fairy vanished.

But Merryweather still had a gift to give. She tried to undo the curse by saying these words to the baby:
"If through this evil fairy's trick
A spindle should your finger prick,
Not in death, but just in sleep
The fateful prophecy you'll keep.
And from this slumber you shall wake
When True Love's Kiss the spell shall break."

But King Stefan still feared Maleficent's curse. He ordered
every spinning wheel in the land be burned. Then, he and
the good fairies hatched a plan. The fairies would disguise
themselves as peasants and take Aurora to live with them,
deep in the woods, safe from Maleficent, until her sixteenth
birthday.

King Stefan and the Queen watched with heavy hearts as their only child disappeared into the night. They knew it was for the best, but they would miss her.

The years came and went, and the princess grew up safe from the evil curse.

In the woods, a beautiful and happy girl named Briar Rose greeted the day from her cottage window. She did not know she was really the princess Aurora and her "aunties" were the good fairies.

Inside, the three fairies whispered together. It was the girl's sixteenth birthday. They wanted to surprise her with a cake, a new dress . . . and the truth about her royal identity.

The fairies gave Briar Rose a basket and asked her to pick berries in the forest. Then they set to work preparing her surprise.

But even after doing things without magic for sixteen years, the fairies still had trouble baking and sewing. While Flora and Merryweather struggled to make a dress, Fauna wondered how exactly someone folded eggs into cake batter. Finally, the fairies gave up and used their wands. Their magic flew up the chimney, catching the attention of Maleficent's raven, which was flying past.

In the woods, Briar Rose confessed to her animal friends that she had met a handsome prince . . . but only in her dreams. "They say if you dream a thing more than once," she sighed, "it's sure to come true. And I've seen him so many times!"

Briar Rose began to dance with the animals, pretending they were her prince.

A young prince was passing by and heard Briar Rose
humming. He snuck up on the girl and began to dance
with her.

Briar Rose was startled, but the prince somehow
seemed familiar.

The two gazed into each other's eyes, falling deeply
in love.

At the cottage, the fairies gave Briar Rose her birthday surprises. But Briar Rose was distracted. She told her aunts about the boy she had met in the woods.

The fairies knew it was time to tell Briar Rose the truth. She was a princess, betrothed at birth to a prince. And it was time for her to return home.

Devastated, Aurora followed the fairies through the woods, still wishing for her handsome stranger.

Inside the castle, the fairies led Aurora to her room. But when they left, a glowing green ball appeared. In a trance, Aurora followed the light.

Aurora found herself in a room with a spinning wheel and a spindle!

Maleficent's voice filled the room and the evil fairy appeared. "Touch the spindle. Touch it, I say!"

Aurora obeyed.

The three good fairies rushed to the rescue, but they were too late. Aurora had touched the sharp spindle and instantly fallen into a deep sleep. Maleficent's curse had come true.

With a harsh laugh, the evil fairy vanished.

The good fairies wept. "Poor King Stefan and the Queen," said Fauna.

"They'll be heartbroken when they find out," said Merryweather.

"They're not going to," said Flora. "We'll put them all to sleep until the princess awakens."

So the three fairies brought the princess back to her room, then flew above the kingdom, casting a dreamlike spell over everyone in the castle.

Meanwhile, Maleficent had captured the boy Aurora
had fallen in love with, and chained him deep in her
dungeon.

When the fairies arrived to rescue him, they were
surprised to learn that he was none other than Prince
Phillip! The good fairies magically melted Phillip's chains.
They armed him with the Shield of Virtue and the Sword
of Truth and sent him racing to the castle to awaken the
princess.

Maleficent tried to stop Phillip. She hurled heavy boulders at him, but the brave prince rode on.

When he reached Aurora's castle, Maleficent caused a forest of thorns to grow all around it. Phillip hacked the thorns aside with his powerful sword.

In a rage, the evil fairy soared to the top of the highest tower. There she changed into a monstrous dragon. "Now you shall deal with me, oh Prince!" she shrieked. "And all the powers of evil!"

Maleficent breathed huge waves of fire. Phillip ducked behind his strong shield.

Thunder cracked! Flames roared around him! The prince fought bravely. Guided by the good fairies, he flung his magic sword straight as an arrow. It buried itself deep in the dragon's evil heart. Maleficent was no more.

Phillip raced to the tower where his love lay sleeping. He gently kissed her. As Aurora's eyes slowly opened, the whole kingdom awoke.

The king and Queen were overjoyed to see their daughter again.

Wedding plans were soon made, and everyone lived happily ever after!

Aurora's Royal Wedding

Prince Phillip had awoken Princess Aurora from a magical sleep. The two had met in the forest and fallen in love. Aurora had dreamed of marrying the prince. Now, at last, the day was almost here.

Word of the royal wedding spread far and wide.
It was the biggest announcement since Aurora's
homecoming. With the wedding celebration only
a day away, the kingdom set off to prepare.

Prince Phillip made sure Samson had a bath by promising him an extra bucket of oats and a few carrots.

Even King Hubert and King Stefan found a job
to do: tasting treats.

"Everything seems well in hand, Your Majesty," said Flora.
The Queen smiled. "Yes, it does, and I couldn't be more delighted to have my daughter home. I'll leave you now, Aurora, to enjoy the fun of choosing a dress."

"Thank you, Mother," said Aurora, but she was feeling nervous. She had yet to make any royal decisions.

As the Queen exited, the dressmakers burst in.

"These dresses are all so lavish," said Aurora, "they'll barely fit in the closet!"

"If I may, Princess," said one of the dressmakers. "We'll only need to remove your old clothes to make room."

But those were the clothes Princess Aurora had worn when she was hiding in the forest as Briar Rose, just before she discovered the truth that she was a princess.

"What is it, dear?" asked Fauna.

Aurora sighed. "I don't know how to be a princess. What if I'm not a very good one?"

"Nonsense," said Merryweather. "Why, you'll make the finest princess this kingdom has ever seen."

Still, Aurora wasn't so sure.

When Prince Phillip came by later, he had a splendid idea. "Would you like to go for a walk to get away from the wedding planning for a bit?"

"Oh, that would be wonderful!" said Aurora.

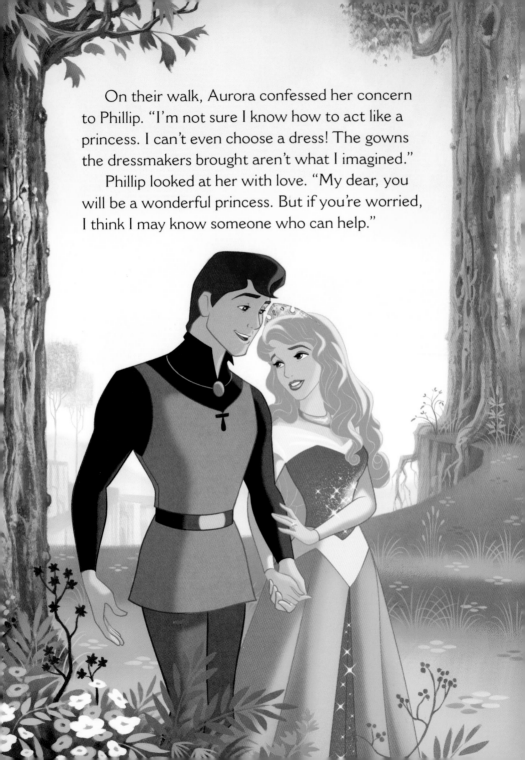

On their walk, Aurora confessed her concern to Phillip. "I'm not sure I know how to act like a princess. I can't even choose a dress! The gowns the dressmakers brought aren't what I imagined."

Phillip looked at her with love. "My dear, you will be a wonderful princess. But if you're worried, I think I may know someone who can help."

Back at the palace, Flora had a plan. "Let's use our wands!"

"Magic won't help," said Fauna. "We don't know how to be a princess."

"Even if we did," Merryweather grumbled, "Aurora has to feel princess-y on the inside."

Flora paused. "We should ask the Queen!"

The good fairies searched the castle. Soon enough, they found the Queen—but Prince Phillip was already with her.

"You see, Your Majesty," he was saying, "I think she would appreciate some help—some reassurance from you, her mother."

The fairies smiled. Phillip was indeed a perfect husband for their Briar Rose.

All together, they led the Queen to Aurora.

"Dear Aurora, I understand that you are worried, but being a princess isn't about what you do. Rather, it's about who you are. A princess is honest, compassionate, intelligent, and kind. And there is no doubt you are all of these things."

"Oh, thank you, Mother!" Aurora said. Then she paused. "I just had an idea about a wedding dress. Would it be possible to wear yours?"

The Queen smiled. "I married your father in a simple but beautiful gown. I think it will fit you perfectly."

On the day of the royal wedding, it seemed the entire kingdom was celebrating. While the handsome Prince Phillip waited at the altar, King Stefan walked Aurora down the aisle. She looked every bit a princess in her mother's dress—and she was starting to feel like one, too.

"Do you, Prince Phillip, take Princess Aurora as your wife?"

"I do."

"Do you, Princess Aurora, take Prince Phillip as your husband?"

"I do."

After the ceremony, the royal couple greeted their guests at the reception and shared a piece of the magnificent wedding cake.

Then it it was time for their first dance. As they twirled
and glided across the royal hall, Aurora felt as if she were
dancing on air. She was surrounded by true friends—and
no evil fairies had sprung up unannounced. Even the good
fairies had behaved, resisting the urge to change Aurora's
wedding dress to pink or blue.

The royal wedding was exactly as Princess
Aurora had imagined . . . once upon a dream.

Aurora's Slumber Party

rincess Aurora loved being married to Prince Phillip and living at the castle. But she missed her fairy friends Flora, Fauna, and Merryweather.

One day Phillip told her he had to visit another kingdom overnight. "Why don't you invite the three good fairies to keep you company while I'm gone," he said.

Flora, Fauna, and Merryweather were excited to be invited to the castle. When they arrived, Aurora was wearing her nightgown.

"Surprise!" Aurora cried. "It's a sleepover! You'd better change into your nightgowns, too."

The good fairies quickly changed into their nightgowns and then used their magic to fill the room with music.

Aurora took each fairy by the hand and whirled her left and right. As she twirled Fauna, Aurora's nightgown suddenly turned a lovely shade of blue.

"Oh, no. That won't do at all," Flora said. She pointed her wand at Aurora and turned her nightgown pink.

Back and forth the nightgown went until finally it settled back to its usual color.

Suddenly, Flora picked up a pillow and swung it at Merryweather. Merryweather ducked and grabbed a pillow of her own. Fauna and Aurora stopped dancing and watched the two fairies. Then they looked at each other and grabbed their own pillows to join the fun.

Soon the room was covered in feathers, and the friends were out of breath from laughing.

All the fighting made everyone hungry, and they went downstairs to make a snack. Merryweather waved her wand, and a stack of triple-decker berry sandwiches appeared. When Flora bit into hers, a dollop of cream flew across the room, right onto Aurora's face!

"Oops," Flora said. "I'm sorry, Princess."

But Aurora wasn't upset. In fact, she was laughing. Sleepovers were all about having fun, and she was having a great time!

"Let's read a story," Aurora suggested when she and
the fairies went back upstairs. She and her friends gathered
around the bed, and Flora read to them. Soon the fairies
began to grow sleepy. Flora set the book aside and they all
crawled into their beds.

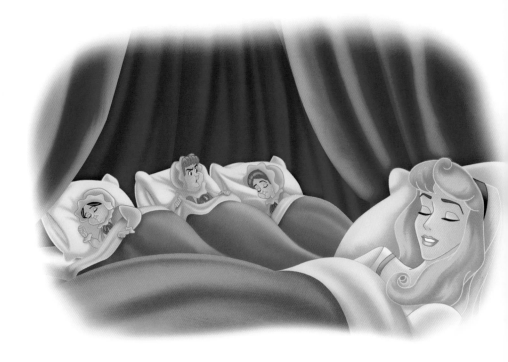

　　In no time, Fauna, Merryweather, and Aurora were fast asleep. But Flora couldn't sleep. She was still too excited from the night.

　　She tossed and turned. She flipped and flopped. And then she accidentally bonked Merryweather on the head!

Merryweather woke up and rubbed her head. "Ouch!" she cried. "Why did you hit me?"

"I didn't mean to," said Flora. "It's just that I can't fall asleep!"

"Well, now I can't sleep, either," said Merryweather.

All their chatter woke up Fauna, who suggested that they try counting sheep to fall asleep.

Flora and Merryweather agreed that Fauna's suggestion was worth trying. They lay down again to count sheep.

"One, two, three . . ." Flora started to count, but all of a sudden her sheep turned blue!

"Twelve, thirteen, fourteen . . ." Merryweather counted her blue sheep. But just when she had almost fallen asleep, her sheep changed from blue to pink. "Blue!" she cried, and changed them back.

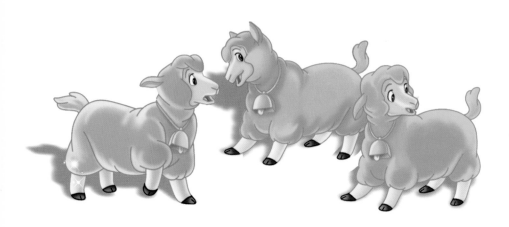

"Pink!" Flora said, and the sheep changed color again.

Soon the two fairies were sitting up and having another argument. But this time they woke Fauna *and* Aurora.

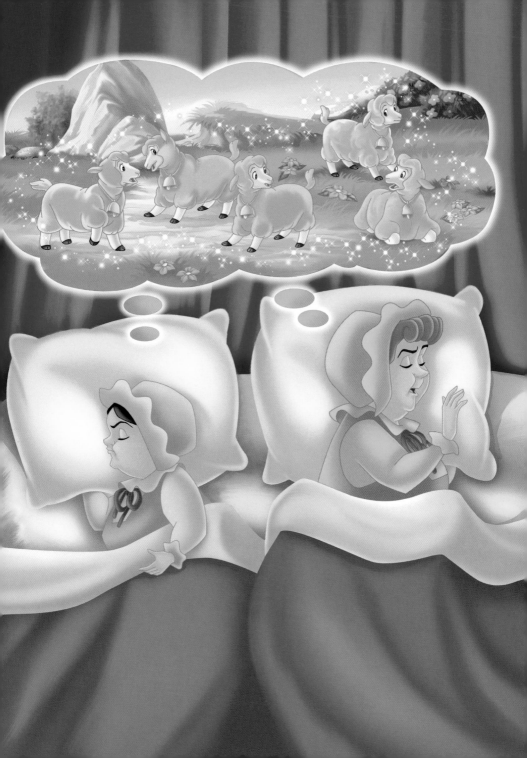

Aurora asked what was wrong, and the fairies told her about the pink and blue sheep. "Maybe there's a better way to fall asleep," she said. Aurora sat up and began to sing a lullaby to the fairies.

As her sweet voice carried across the room, the good fairies closed their eyes. Soon they were all fast asleep. Even Flora!

"Ah, that's better," Aurora said. And then, humming the lullaby softly to herself, she pulled up the covers and went back to sleep.

Aurora and the
Helpful Dragon

urora and Phillip were out for a ride when Aurora
spotted a small dragon behind a tree.

"Oh, he's so cute!" she exclaimed as she dismounted.

"Grrgrrgrr?" the little dragon murmured, clambering into
Aurora's lap.

"I think he's saying he's not dangerous," Aurora laughed.
"Please, let's take him home. I'm going to name him Crackle!"

Aurora's horse tossed her mane and pawed the ground. She was afraid of the dragon. Crackle's tail drooped sadly. Then he grinned a funny little grin. Suddenly, he licked the horse's nose with his long, warm tongue. Aurora's horse blinked with surprise and nuzzled Crackle under the chin. The little dragon giggled.

When Phillip and Aurora rode into the courtyard, the three fairies were hanging banners for King Stefan and the Queen, who were coming for a ball that night.

Flora gasped when she saw Crackle. "Dragons can be dangerous."

"Remember the last one!" Fauna added.

"Oooh, I think he's sweet," Merryweather spoke up.

"Grrrgrr," Crackle babbled.

"He thinks you're sweet, too," Aurora told Merryweather.

Just then, Crackle noticed a kitten in Fauna's workbasket.

Crackle listened to the cute kitten purring. Then he scrunched up his mouth and closed his eyes.

"Purrgrr, purrgrr!" Crackle tried to purr. Clouds of smoke puffed from his nose and mouth.

"*Aachoo! Aachooooie! Ah-ah-ah-CHOO!*" The fairies sneezed so hard that they fluttered backward.

"Please—*achoo*—stop trying to purr!" Fauna exclaimed.

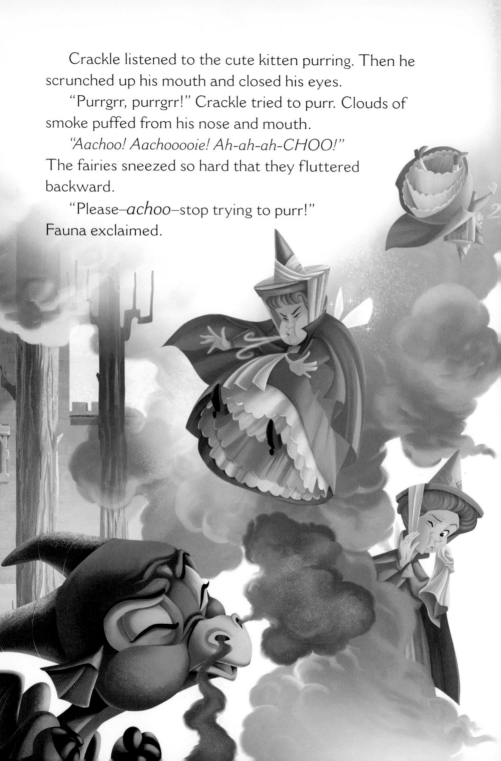

Crackle looked sad for a moment. Then he saw the kitten playing with a ball of yarn from the workbasket, and his eyes lit up. He snatched a ball of yarn with his mouth. *Whoosh!*—it caught fire. Merryweather put the fire out with her wand.

"Oh, Crackle," Aurora said gently. "You're not a kitten. You're a dragon."

Crackle's lower lip trembled.

Aurora carried Crackle into the castle and cuddled him on a window seat. A bird was singing outside. Crackle's ears perked up and his eyes shone hopefully.

"LAAAlaagrr!" he bellowed.

King Hubert heard the racket and rushed into the room.

"Oh, my, my, my! How did a dragon get in here?" he blustered.

Frightened by the king, Crackle jumped from the window seat and ran into the garden. Aurora ran after him. At last she found the little dragon sitting beside a waterfall that splashed down from one pool to another. Crackle was studying a fish swimming in the lowest pool.

Before Aurora could stop him, Crackle splashed into the water. The startled fish leaped into a higher pool.

"Crackle, you're not a fish!" Aurora exclaimed as she pulled Crackle from the pool. "You're not a kitten, or a dog, or a bird, either. You're a dragon!"

Tears rolled down Crackle's face. "Grrgrrgrr," he sobbed. Suddenly, Aurora understood.

"Do you think no one will like you because you're a dragon?" she asked.

Crackle nodded and whimpered sadly.

"Crackle, you can't change being a dragon," Aurora said kindly. "But you don't have to be a dangerous dragon. You can be a brave, helpful dragon."

Crackle stopped crying. "Grrgrrgrrgrr?" he growled hopefully.

Before Aurora could answer, thunder boomed. Wind blew black clouds over the sun. Aurora snatched up Crackle. She reached the castle doors just as the rain began to pour down.

Everyone was gathered in the grand hallway, watching the storm.

"I'm afraid King Stefan and the Queen might lose their way on the road above the cliffs," Prince Phillip said, his voice filled with concern. "I should ride out to help."

Aurora looked at Crackle. "Do you want to show everyone that you're a brave and helpful dragon?" she asked.

"GRRRgrrrgrr!" Crackle exclaimed enthusiastically.

"Fly to the top of the highest castle tower," Aurora said. "Then blow the largest, brightest flames you can."

Soon gold-and-red light flashed up into the sky above the watchtower.

Again and again, Crackle blew his flames until, at last, Phillip shouted. "I see King Stefan and the Queen! They're almost here!"

Everyone hurried to greet the visiting royals.

"The tower light saved us!" King Stefan exclaimed. "I need one like it!"

At that moment Crackle flew happily to join in the fun.

"Well, there he is! Our new tower light," King Hubert said with a laugh.

"A dragon?" King Stefan asked.

"But dragons are danger—"

"Not Crackle," Aurora interrupted.

"He's a brave and helpful dragon!"

That night at the ball, Crackle lit the candles, warmed food, and kept the fireplace blazing. King Hubert and the fairies were so pleased that they took turns scratching Crackle beneath his chin.

As Prince Phillip and Aurora danced, Crackle trotted beside them. Outside, it was cold and stormy. But inside, everyone was happy and warm— especially Crackle the helpful dragon.

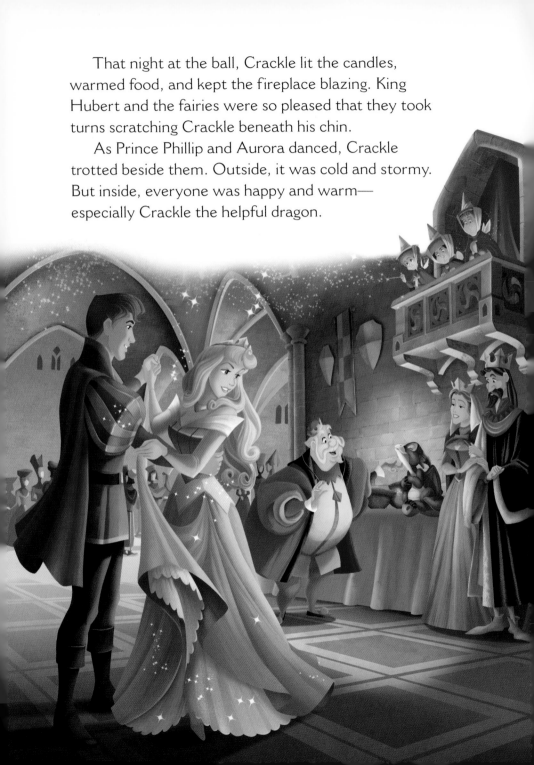

Buttercup
the Brave

urora loved living at the palace. But she missed the little cottage in the woods where she had grown up. One morning, she had an idea. She would take her horse, Buttercup, out to see the good fairies at the cottage.

"Why don't you let me saddle up Samson and come with you?" Phillip suggested, looking worried. "You shouldn't ride off through the woods all alone."

"Don't be silly," Aurora said with a laugh. "I grew up in those woods, remember? Besides, I won't be alone. I'll be with Buttercup. He'll take care of me!"

Aurora and Buttercup pranced off across the grounds. But the moment they entered the woods, Buttercup became a different horse. His steps slowed to a crawl. His eyes bulged nervously. And when some of Aurora's little woodland friends appeared, Buttercup tried to spin around and run away!

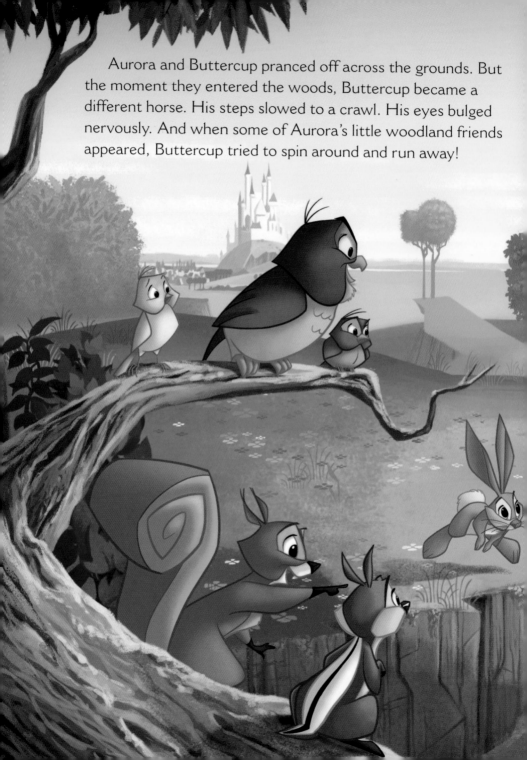

"What's the matter, Buttercup?" Aurora exclaimed in surprise. "Why, there's nothing to be frightened of!"

She could hardly believe the change in her horse. He was even afraid to step over a branch on the trail.

And when she asked him to walk
through a forest stream, he nearly fainted!

By the time she reached the cottage, Aurora was feeling a bit frustrated. How could a horse who was so brave at the palace be so timid in the woods?

Flora, Fauna, and Merryweather hurried out of their cottage. "Oh, what a lovely pony!" Merryweather exclaimed.

"Yes, he's beautiful, dear," Fauna added.

Aurora sighed. "He *is* beautiful," she said. "But he seems to be afraid of everything in the woods!"

"There, there." Flora smiled. "I'm sure it will be all right. You'll just need to be patient with him, that's all."

"Yes, dear, be patient," Merryweather agreed. But she sounded distracted. She moved closer to get a better look at Buttercup. "What a nice coat he has!"

"And such shiny hooves," Fauna added.

"Though he might look even nicer if his hooves were blue," Merryweather mused.

Zap! She aimed her wand. Just like that, Buttercup's hooves turned blue!

"Oh, don't be silly!" Flora exclaimed. "A horse shouldn't have blue hooves. On the other hand, his coat might look prettier in pink. . . ."

Zap! Buttercup's hooves returned to their normal color. But the rest of him turned pink.

"Quit that!" Merryweather cried. "Blue!"

"Pink!" Flora argued back.

Zap! Zap!

As the two fairies fought, the horse changed from one color to the next. Buttercup looked confused.

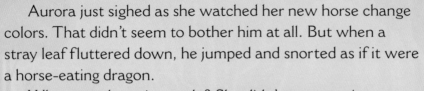

Aurora just sighed as she watched her new horse change colors. That didn't seem to bother him at all. But when a stray leaf fluttered down, he jumped and snorted as if it were a horse-eating dragon.

What was she going to do? She didn't want to give up on him. Buttercup was perfect in every other way. Why did he have to be so skittish in the forest?

Soon it was time to say good-bye to the fairies. Aurora did her best to ignore how Buttercup jumped and cringed at every shadow and leaf along the way.

Aurora was so deep in thought that she wasn't paying attention to anything else. But she looked up when Buttercup suddenly stopped dead in his tracks.

"What is it *this* time?" she asked with a sigh.

Then Aurora looked at the trail ahead . . . and gasped in horror. An enormous mountain lion was blocking their path!

Oh, no! Aurora's heart raced with fright as she watched the creature creep closer.

To Aurora's surprise, Buttercup didn't panic or try to run. Instead, he stood proudly and puffed himself up to look even bigger than he was. He planted his hooves and snorted angrily at the mountain lion.

Then he marched forward and struck out at the lion
with his front hooves! Aurora hung on. She was still
scared. But it seemed that Buttercup wasn't!

When the mountain lion didn't budge, Buttercup leaped forward and pinned its tail to the ground with one hoof. Aurora grabbed a branch and gave the lion a smart rap on the nose.

The lion didn't like that at all. It let out an
embarrassed yowl. Then it yanked its tail free and
raced away into the woods.

Aurora was pleased with herself—and with her horse.

"Come on, Buttercup," she said, giving him a pat. "Let's go home."

Buttercup snorted again, proudly, and pranced off. But as they neared the castle, a butterfly fluttered past. Buttercup's eyes widened, and he jumped in terror.

But this time, Aurora just smiled. "You helped me feel brave when it was most important, Buttercup," she told him. "Now maybe I can help you get past your fears, too."

Aurora stroked Buttercup's neck and talked to him in a soft voice, reminding him to stay calm. The butterfly fluttered closer and closer . . . and finally landed right on his nose (which was only shaking a *little*).

"Good boy!" she praised him. "You know, Buttercup, I think we make a perfect team!"

A Moment to Remember

$\mathcal{P}$rincess Aurora sighed. She loved Prince Phillip, but life in the palace was so very busy. That night there would be some more royal visitors. The palace staff had been working for days to get ready.

Aurora looked out the window. The courtyard below reminded her of the glade where she had met Prince Phillip. Things had been so much simpler there. Aurora sighed again.

"You see, Merryweather?" said Fauna. "I told you Aurora didn't want to wear that dress. This one will look much better." Fauna gestured at the gown Aurora would wear that night and it turned pink. As soon as Fauna turned her back, Merryweather tried to make the dress blue.

"Now, dears," said Flora, "let's not argue. The dress should look however Aurora wants. What do you think, dear?"

Before Aurora could answer, the Royal Chef entered the
room to show her the ice sculpture for the evening.

The sculpture looked like a swan. Aurora smiled to tell the
chef that she approved. But no sooner had he turned away
than one of the castle maids came to see her.

"Princess Aurora, we're almost out of candles, and I don't
know where we'll find more on such short notice!"

Aurora reminded the maid to check the lower storeroom.

As the maid left, Prince Phillip came into the room. "Hello, dearest," he said.

Aurora held out her hands. Phillip's loving gaze made her forget all her worries. "Oh, Phillip, I'm so glad to see you. I—"

"Ahem." The Royal Florist cleared his throat. "Princess Aurora, could you please tell the Royal Table Setter that she must place flowers in the middle of each table tonight?"

"Princess Aurora," said the Royal Table Setter, "could you please tell the Royal Florist that our guests will never see one another if I put his big flower arrangements in the middle of each table?"

"Why don't you just put a single flower on each table?" said Aurora.

The two servants looked at her, horrified. "A single flower?" they said. "The king would be so insulted!"

"Pardon me, Princess Aurora," the Royal Steward interrupted.
"But I must have your approval on the seating arrangements."

"Thank you, Steward," said Princess Aurora. "I will look at
them—"

"As soon as we return," Prince Phillip finished.

Both Aurora and the Steward looked at Phillip in surprise.

"Where are we going, Phillip?" Aurora asked.

Phillip smiled. "Out for a ride where no one can ask us anything."

Aurora changed into her riding clothes, and the two set off. "Oh Phillip, this was such a good idea," Aurora said. "It will be so nice to have some time alone to—"

Just then, horns blared, and a group of ten riders trotted over to Phillip and Aurora.

"The Royal Equestrian Guard, reporting for duty, Prince Phillip," said the Head Guardsman.

Aurora looked down, trying to hide her disappointment. Then she noticed Phillip's horse, Samson. Aurora bent and whispered to Samson. Then she gave him a light pat. Samson whinnied and lifted his head. Before Phillip could stop him, Samson charged away from the palace.

Aurora and her horse dashed after them, leaving the Royal Equestrians far behind.

Phillip and Aurora galloped through the field and into the woods. Suddenly Samson left the forest path and stopped short.

SPLASH! Phillip sailed over Samson's head and landed in a shallow stream.

"No carrots for you, boy!" Prince Phillip scolded his horse. He looked up and saw Aurora. She slid out of the saddle and smiled down at him.

"Do you remember this place, Phillip?" Aurora asked.

Phillip sloshed out of the stream and sat down on a rock. He pulled off his boots and dumped water out of them.

Aurora took off her shoes. She spun around gracefully, humming a tune.

"Yes," Prince Phillip said softly. "I remember this place. . . ."

He joined Aurora, and they danced once again in the glade where they had met.

"I will never forget that day," said Aurora, "no matter how busy our lives become."

Prince Phillip smiled and touched her face. "Nor will I. For when I am with you, all others disappear."

Aurora laughed quietly. She wished she could bring the peace and love they had known in the glade back to the palace.

All too soon, it was time to go back to the
castle. As Aurora climbed into her horse's saddle,
an idea formed. If she worked quickly and
carefully, she could surprise Phillip with it.

Phillip touched Aurora's hand and said,
"You go ahead, dear. I'll be back soon."

Aurora nodded and smiled. Yes, that
would give her plan a head start.

Phillip, meanwhile, had an
idea of his own. "Not a word of
this to the princess," he said to her
animal friends as he gathered some flowers.

Aurora did not see Prince Phillip for the rest of the afternoon. She was too busy working on Phillip's surprise. Servants carried flowers, food, and candles to the tables. Flora, Fauna, and Merryweather flitted about, helping wherever they could.

More than once, Aurora heard a servant murmur, "Our guests will certainly be . . . surprised."

Aurora just smiled. "It's Prince Phillip I want to surprise," she told the servants. "Not a word of this to him."

The servants nodded. Prince Phillip's valet hurried off to keep the prince away from the ballroom.

That night, the good fairies helped Aurora dress.
Suddenly, Prince Phillip came into the room. He held out
a simple crown, made from the flowers of the glade. "Would
you like to wear this, too?" he asked.
"Oh, Phillip!" Aurora put on the flower crown and hugged
her husband. "It is perfect for this evening."

"And now I have a surprise for you!" Aurora led Phillip down the stairs to the ballroom. It was dark and empty.

"You've canceled the ball?" Prince Phillip asked. "Have the guests left?"

"No, Phillip." Aurora touched her flower crown. "You brought our little glade back to me. Now let me take you back to our little glade."

Aurora led Phillip into the courtyard. A sweet breeze whispered through the flowers and trees. Water danced in the fountain with a sound like a stream. Candles flickered in the darkness like the stars above them.

"The glade will always be in our hearts," Aurora whispered. "But now it is in our palace, too."

Just then Phillip's father approached. "This is much better than the stuffy balls I usually attend," he said.

Prince Phillip took Aurora's hand. As the two danced,
they truly felt as if they were back in their magical glade.